The Vikings' Secret Weapon

Written by Ben Hubbard

Illustrated by Emmanuel Cerisier

Contents

Collins

1 Viking attack!

The Viking Age began in 793 CE, when Viking raiders attacked a **monastery** at Lindisfarne, Britain. They murdered many monks there and enslaved others. They then filled their longship with church treasure and sailed home to Scandinavia.

The Vikings were armed with axes and swords, but their secret weapon was the longship. The longship was the most advanced ship in the world: it was sleek, fast and had a shallow bottom to travel up rivers and land on sandy beaches. It used both **oars** and sails so the Vikings could attack at speed. For over 300 years, the Viking longship created terror in Europe and beyond.

Lindisfarne

Britain

2 The Vikings and the sea

The Vikings came from the Scandinavian countries of Denmark, Norway and Sweden. Scandinavia is a region with jagged coastlines, large rivers and winding **inlets** called fjords. The sea has always been central to the people who live there.

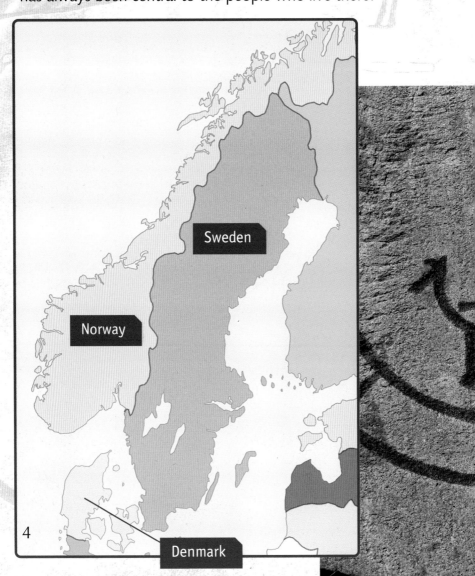

Sweden

Norway

Denmark

The Scandinavian countries were not united, but by the 700s they shared a similar way of life, language and beliefs. It was around this time that warriors built the first longships to sail abroad to fight, trade and **raid**. They described these trips as going "a viking", which is why they were known as "Vikings".

These rock carvings from Tanum, Sweden were made around 2,100 years ago. They show that Scandinavian boats were used in war hundreds of years before the Viking Age even began.

5

3 The first boats

The first Scandinavian boats were large canoes. They were carved from a single tree trunk with a hollowed-out centre. Later ships were also made in a canoe shape, but with long wooden **planks**. These "plank" ships were how longships were built a few hundred years later.

A reconstruction of the *Hjortspring Boat* based on the actual boat shown on the left.

The *Hjortspring Boat* is Europe's oldest "plank" boat, built around 350 BCE. It was like a small, early longship. Dug up in 1921 in a Danish bog, the *Hjortspring Boat* was built with overlapping planks and had benches inside for 24 oarsmen. Weapons such as axes and bows and arrows were found with it. It was a boat built for war.

4 Building a longship

Longships took at least six months to build. They were designed carefully so that the ships could sail on the roughest waters and carry people long distances.

1. A long **keel** was cut from a single tree trunk.

2. Overlapping planks were attached to the keel and built up along the sides.

3. Floor timbers were placed across the middle of the **hull** and benches added for oarsmen. Holes were cut for oars and a steering oar placed at the back. A **mast** was added.

4. The hull was made watertight with a covering of animal hair and black tar.

5 Made for war

With its armed warriors,
striped sail, and sides
covered in shields, a Viking
longship was a scary sight for
those on shore. A **prow** decorated
with the head of a dragon or
other mythical creature
was sometimes
added to create
extra fear.

steering oar

Fact!

This illustration is partly based on the *Gokstad Ship*,
shown in the photo above, in the Viking Ship Museum,
Norway. This longship could carry 70 warriors and was
24 metres long. That's longer than two buses.

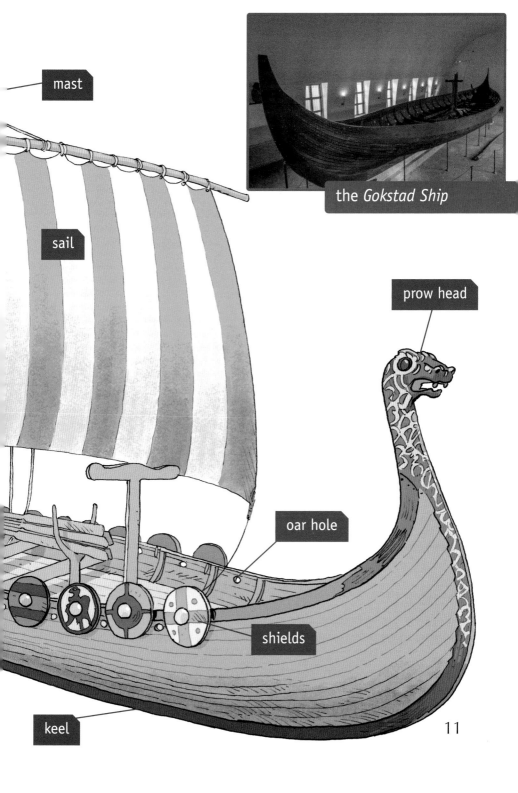

mast

sail

the *Gokstad Ship*

prow head

oar hole

shields

keel

6 The first raids

The first Viking raid on the Lindisfarne Monastery in 793 CE was only the beginning of their attacks. For hundreds of years afterwards, longships targeted monasteries, villages and towns around Britain and Ireland. During the raids, Vikings would kill people, enslave others and steal valuable items.

Fact!

Roskilde 6 was the largest Viking longship ever found. At 36 metres, it was longer than three buses and could carry 80 warriors.

The first raids involved a group of just a few Viking longships, trying their luck. But from the 830s, the Viking attacks were large and organised. In the 860s, whole armies sailed to the shores of Europe, sometimes with dozens of ships. These Vikings were not raiders, but invaders, planning to **settle** in the places they landed.

7 Attack on Paris

Britain and Ireland were not the only countries attacked by Vikings. In 845 CE, an army of 120 longships sailed up the River Seine in France. The Vikings burnt and robbed villages as they travelled towards the country's capital, Paris.

The French king, Charles the Bald, quickly gathered an army, but this was crushed by the Vikings. They entered Paris, killing and stealing as they went. The Vikings set many buildings alight and would not leave Paris until Charles the Bald paid them with gold and silver to go away.

8 Raiders and traders

The Vikings were not only raiders who used their
longships to attack. They also traded valuable items,
such as animal fur, jewellery, walrus skin and rope.
In the 700s, trading towns sprang up around Scandinavia.
Traders from around the world sailed into these harbours
to buy and sell goods.

This engraving was left by the Viking called
Halfdan in Istanbul's Hagia Sophia.

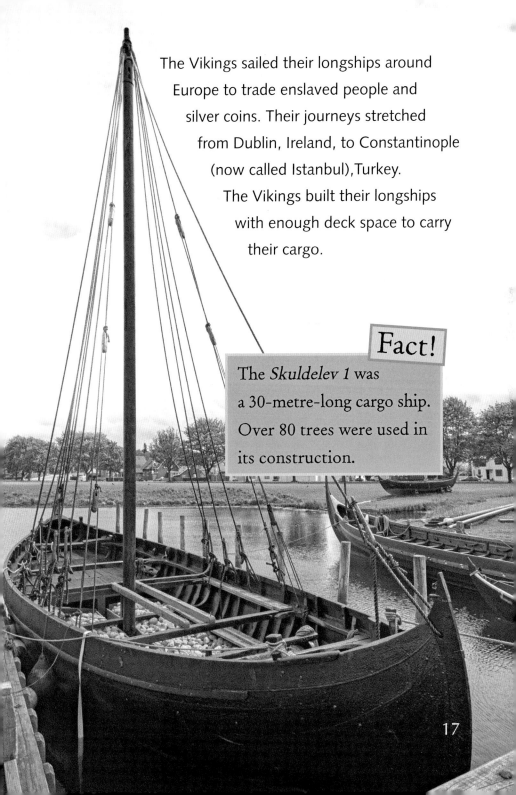

The Vikings sailed their longships around
Europe to trade enslaved people and
silver coins. Their journeys stretched
from Dublin, Ireland, to Constantinople
(now called Istanbul), Turkey.
The Vikings built their longships
with enough deck space to carry
their cargo.

Fact!

The *Skuldelev 1* was
a 30-metre-long cargo ship.
Over 80 trees were used in
its construction.

17

9 Exploration and expansion

The Vikings didn't stop there. Whilst those from Norway and Denmark attacked Western Europe during the 800s, many Swedish Vikings took their longships to raid and trade in Eastern Europe.

They sailed across the Baltic Sea and down rivers towards Constantinople. If a river was too small or too wild for a longship, the Vikings simply dragged and carried it across land. This was called portaging.

10 Invaders, settlers and explorers

By the 800s, the Vikings had spread far and wide. In 865 CE, a great Viking army of over 1000 warriors sailed on longships to invade England. Eventually the English king, Alfred the Great, agreed to let the army settle in a region of England called the Danelaw.

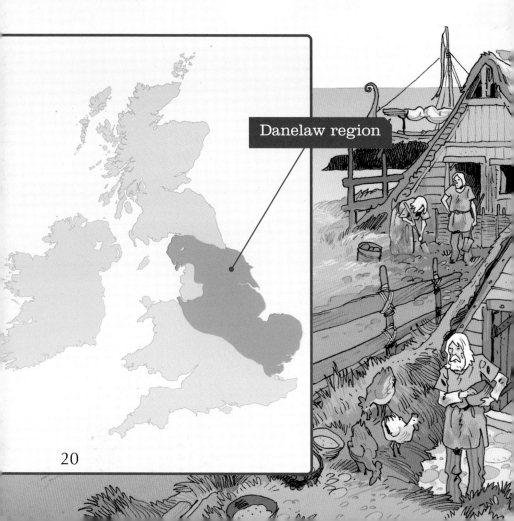

Danelaw region

The Vikings were also explorers. A Viking longship accidentally landed on Iceland around 860 CE while trying to sail to Scotland. Later, Vikings from Iceland settled on Greenland in around 930 CE and landed in Newfoundland, Canada, in 986 CE.

11 Sea battles

Viking longships were not built to ram other ships at sea.
However, sea battles between enemy Vikings did take place.
They sailed their longships towards each other, then fired
arrows and threw spears. Once alongside another longship,
the Vikings leapt from one boat to the other to fight. This was
like battling on land but at sea.

The Battle of Svolder in 999 CE was a famous Viking sea battle between 71 Danish ships and 11 Norwegian ships. Norwegian king Olaf Tryggvason lost the battle and threw himself into the sea so that he wasn't captured.
He was never seen again.

12 Burials

The most important Vikings were buried in the ground with their ships. Others were buried with their weapons. Sometimes, a dead Viking was laid out on a ship, which was set on fire and pushed out to sea.

The *Oseberg Ship* was a famous early longship. It was used for the burial of a Norwegian queen in 834 CE. The queen and her precious objects were all buried with the ship, including combs, clothes and wooden chests.

The stones in burial sites were often laid out in the shape of longships, such as this one in Jutland, Denmark. The graves show the importance of ships to the Vikings, not only in life, but also in death.

13 The Viking end

Around 1066, the Viking Age came to an end. People in Norway, Sweden and Denmark began to think that raiding other countries aboard longships was wrong. Before long, Vikings no longer existed.

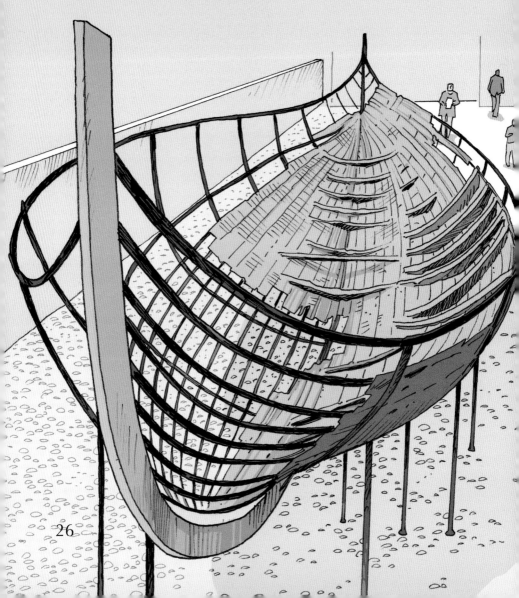

Longships left behind have taught us much about the Vikings.
Some of the ships in this book, including the *Skuldelev 1*
and the *Skuldelev 5*, were found in Denmark's Roskilde Harbour.
Models of such longships can be found around the world,
showing people today what they looked like. The Vikings' secret
weapon – the longship – lives on!

Glossary

hull the main body of a ship

inlets small or narrow bays leading from the sea

keel a piece of supporting wood that runs lengthwise along
the bottom of a ship

mast a long, thick pole that supports a ship's sail

monastery a house where monks live

oars poles with a flat blade to power a boat or ship through
the water

planks flat, thick pieces of wood

prow the bow, or front, of a ship

raid attack by surprise

settle to move and live in a new place

Index

Viking journeys

Greenland

Iceland

Newfoundland

Dublin

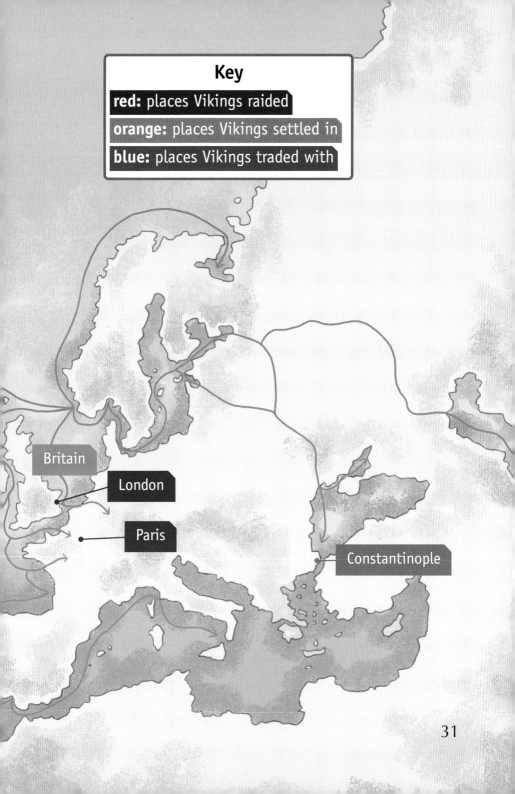

Key

red: places Vikings raided

orange: places Vikings settled in

blue: places Vikings traded with

Britain

London

Paris

Constantinople

 Ideas for reading

Written by Gill Matthews
Primary Literacy Consultant

Reading objectives:

- Ask questions to improve their understanding of a text
- Identify main ideas drawn from more than one paragraph and summarise these
- Retrieve and record information from non-fiction

Spoken language objectives:

- Give well-structured descriptions, explanations and narratives for different purposes, including for expressing feelings
- Speak audibly and fluently with an increasing command of Standard English
- Participate in discussions, presentations, performances, role play, improvisations and debates

Curriculum links: History – Viking and Anglo-Saxon struggle for the Kingdom of England; Geography – Locational knowledge, Geographical skills and fieldwork

Interest words: raiders, traders, exploration, expansion, invaders, settlers, explorers

Build a context for reading

- Show children the front cover, ask them to read the title and look at the illustrations. Discuss what kind of book they think this is. Explore what they think the secret weapon might be.
- Read the back cover blurb. Explore children's existing knowledge of the Vikings and their longships.
- Discuss the features children expect to find in non-fiction books. Ask them to flick through the book and find some of these features.
- Turn to the contents page and ask children how the information is organised (*sequentially*).

Understand and apply reading strategies

- Read pp2–3 aloud to the group. Ask questions that will develop children's scanning skills, e.g. In which year did the Viking Age begin? Where was the monastery that the Vikings attacked?